Space Glop

Space Glop

Written by Nicola Matthews
Illustrated by Eleanor Taylor

Hooked On Phonics

ISBN 1-887942-59-9 First Edition 2 3 4 5 6 7 8 9 10

Contents

Special Words

Special words help make this story fun.
Your child may need help reading them.

eyes

flower

house

seat

slime

1. Mess, Mess, Mess!

Jazz's spaceship is a mess. Jazz is a space kid, and space kids do not like messes.

Zug, the space bug, likes messes. He likes space slugs and frogs too.

The frogs jump all over the spaceship and track in mud. The slugs get slime all over the rug and all over Jazz's things.

Jazz can get rid of the mud and the slime. Jazz can catch jumping frogs and slugs too. Jazz gets her net and jumps after them.

Zug makes a big mess when he eats. He drops space glop on Jazz's bed. He drops red jam on Jazz's best rug. Jazz does not want space glop on her bed

or red jam on her space rug.
So she gets her brush and her
dust pan and her dust rag. She
gets rid of the red jam, but she
can’t get rid of the space glop.

“What is the problem, Jazz?” says Zug.

"This ship is a mess," says Jazz, "and we have run out of space suds. I need space suds to get rid of the space glop."

"I like space glop in my bed," says Zug.

"Well, I do not," says Jazz. "We will need to go to planet Igg to get space suds, and that's that."

"Can Polly and Max come too?" asks Zug.

"OK," says Jazz. "That will be fun. Let's go pick them up in the spaceship. Then we can go get the space suds."

Jazz gets in her seat and puts on her seat belt. Zug gets in his seat and puts on his seat belt.

"Get set for liftoff! Flip the switch, Zug!" says Jazz.

"Oh, no!" says Zug.

Oh, no!

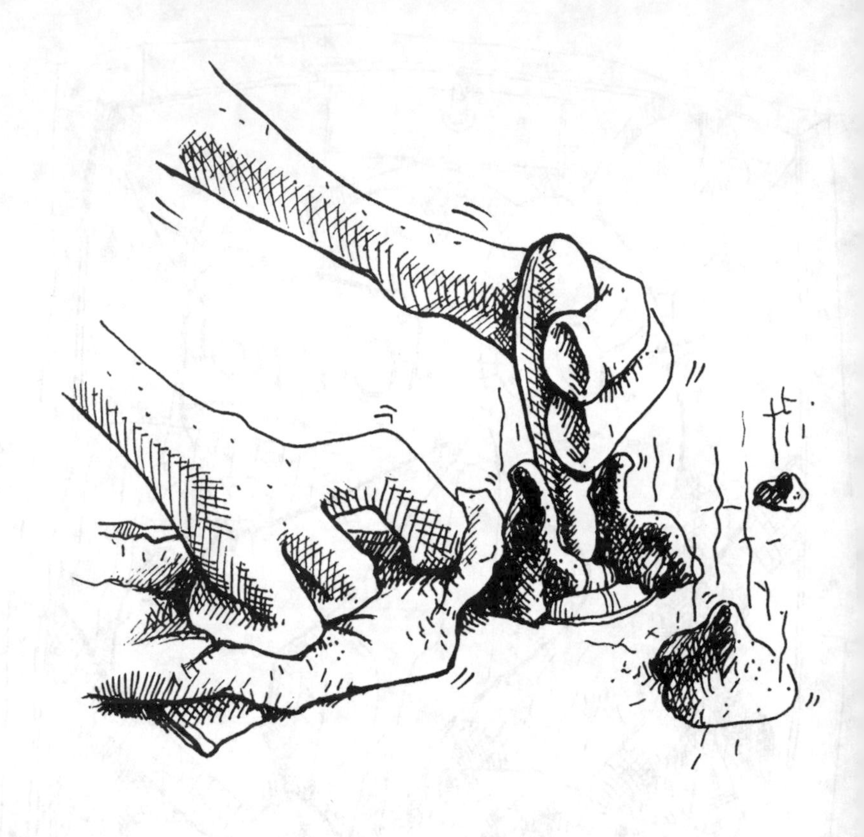

The switch is stuck! There is glop on it. Jazz gets her dust rag. She rubs the switch, but it is still stuck!

Zug pecks the switch, but it is still stuck!

Jazz lets the frogs jump on it. She tells the slugs to put slime all over it, but it is still stuck!

“Well,” says Jazz, “we will just have to forget the spaceship and go in the blast box!”

B.B.1

The blast box does not work too well.

"Oh, no!" says Zug.

2. Where Are We?

"OK, let's go!" says Jazz. She shuts her eyes and thinks about Max's house. That's how the blast box works. It can go wherever Jazz wants it to.

The blast box begins to buzz, then—ZIP!—the blast box blasts off—and lands with a crash in Max's shed.

"That was not a good landing!" says Zug crossly.

Zug gets up and flaps his wings.
"I do not like this blast box!"
he says.

Jazz gets out of the blast box to have a look.

"This does not look like Max's house," she says.

Zug gets out too. “No, it does not!” he says.

Jazz says, “It can’t be Max’s house. Mom and Max and Polly are not here!”

"This is not Max's house," says Zug. "It's a shed!"

"Oh, no!" says Jazz.

"Oh, yes!" says Zug.
YAP! YAP! YAP!
They look and see Polly.

“Help! Polly!” yells Zug.

“Get Max and Mom!” yells Jazz. “We are stuck in the shed!”

Max and Mom are there in a flash. Mom unlocks the shed.

“Why are you in the shed?” she asks.

Jazz tells Mom about the blast box, but Mom does not look. Polly is in her flower beds.

"Do not dig up my flowers!" Mom yells, and she runs off.

Jazz tells Max why they need to go on a trip to space.

Max asks Mom, “Mom, can I go with Jazz? She needs to get some things to fix up the spaceship.”

Mom does not know he wants to go in a blast box.

"OK, but be back at six. I am glad you have something to do," she says.

"Polly can go with you too. I do not want her in my flower beds," says Mom. "Have fun and be good!"

Mom does not see Max, Zug, Polly, and Jazz go in the shed. She does not see them get in the blast box. She does not know that Zug says, "Oh, no!"

That's a good thing!

3. Space Suds!

The blast box is not very big. Zug has to sit on top of Jazz. Polly has to sit on Max's lap.

"OK, let's go!" says Jazz. She shuts her eyes and thinks about planet Igg. That where she gets space suds.

The blast box begins to buzz,
then—ZIP! It blasts off and…

. . . lands with a crash on
planet Igg.

“Not a good landing!” says Zug.

“No kidding,” says Max.

“YAP!” says Polly.

"What a fuss!" says Jazz. "Now let's go and get the space suds!"

The blast box has landed by a lot of trees that have big flowers on them. The flowers look like balls, and they smell like candy. The grass looks just like pink cotton candy.

"I like this planet," says Max.

Jazz picks some flowers from the trees and puts them in her bag. Polly and Zug want to play ball with one of them.

Zug kicks the ball, and Polly grabs it with her fangs.

“Do not do that!” yells Jazz.

But that’s when the big flower pops, and the suds get all over Polly and Zug.

Now the pets have suds all over them.

"This stuff smells!" says Zug.

"Yuck!" says Max.

“What is this stuff?” asks Max.
“Space suds,” says Jazz. “Space suds stick to space glop. That’s how we get rid of space glop.

Now we have to get back to the blast box fast, or Polly and Zug will stick to the grass."

The pets quickly get into the blast box. Jazz and Max get in too. They do not want the pets to sit on them, but the blast box is not big.

“Let’s go now, or we will all get stuck to the blast box,” says Jazz. The space suds drip off Zug’s wings and down Jazz’s neck. Space suds drip off Polly onto her leg.

Jazz shuts her eyes and thinks of the spaceship. The blast box begins to buzz, then—ZIP!

The blast box blasts off and lands with a crash by Jazz's spaceship.

4. Stuck!

The blast box is down, but Jazz can't get out.

Jazz is stuck to Zug. Zug is stuck to Polly. Polly is stuck to Max, and Max is stuck to the blast box.

“Oh, no!” says Zug.

“What do we do now?” asks Max. He can’t lift his feet. They are stuck.

It is not much fun in the blast box.

"We need a plan," says Zug.

"We need a plan," says Max.

Jazz grins. "I have a plan, but you will not like it."

Jazz shuts her eyes and thinks... she thinks of the pond.

The blast box begins to buzz, then—ZIP!

The blast box blasts off—and lands with a PLOP in the pond. Max yells. Polly yaps. And Zug yells too.

"Why did you do that, Jazz?" they ask.

"Space suds do not stick when they are wet," she says. "Now I am not stuck to Zug, who is not stuck to Polly, who is not stuck to Max. And Max is not stuck to the blast box. We can all get out now."

Then Polly begins to wag, and Max gets even wetter!

"Now what?" asks Max.

"I have just three space sud flowers left in my bag," says Jazz.

“My blast box has sunk to the bottom of the pond. And I still have to get rid of the mess in my spaceship!”

Jazz and Max and Zug and Polly all go into the spaceship.

"I cannot fix my blast box. It will never blast off now," says Jazz. "And my ship is still a mess."

Max looks at the ship. "We will help you get rid of the mess," he says.

Jazz gets out the space suds.

Max gets the brush. Polly puts on the dust rag. Zug gets the dust pan. Then quick as a flash, the spaceship is all fixed up.

“I know!” says Zug. “The blast box is still in the pond. Let’s let the fish play in it.”

"That's good!" says Jazz. "The fish will like it! Zug! Come here. I need you! I have a plan. . . ."

"Oh, no!" says Zug.

"Oh, yes!" says Jazz. "Let's make a new blast box!"